81757

E   Jonas, Ann.
              Round trip / by Ann Jonas. -- New
            York : Greenwillow Books, [1983]
              p. cm.

              Summary:
                Black and white illustrations and
            text record the sights on a day trip
            to the city and back home again to the
            country.
                ISBN 0-688-01772-X : $8.00. -- ISBN
            0-688-01781-9 (lib. bdg.) : $7.63

              1. Cities and towns--Fiction. 2.
            Country life--Fiction. I. Title.

SAN RAF   840717   840717
C000293   /NBG   83-B10352
JONRTRI   1874-6313   82-12026/AC

ROUND TRIP

ANN JONAS

GREENWILLOW BOOKS, NEW YORK

Library of Congress Cataloging in
Publication Data

Jonas, Ann. Round trip.

Summary: Black and white illustrations and
text record the sights on a day trip to the city
and back home again to the country.
[1. Cities and towns—Fiction.
2. Country life—Fiction]
I. Title.
PZ7.J664Ro 1983   [E]   82-12026
ISBN 0-688-01772-X
ISBN 0-688-01781-9 (lib. bdg.)

For Don Nina Amy

We started out as soon as it was light.

Our neighborhood was quiet, the houses dark.
The sun shone on the pond.

Town was empty,
the stores still closed.

We passed a small farm in the valley,

We passed smoky factories.

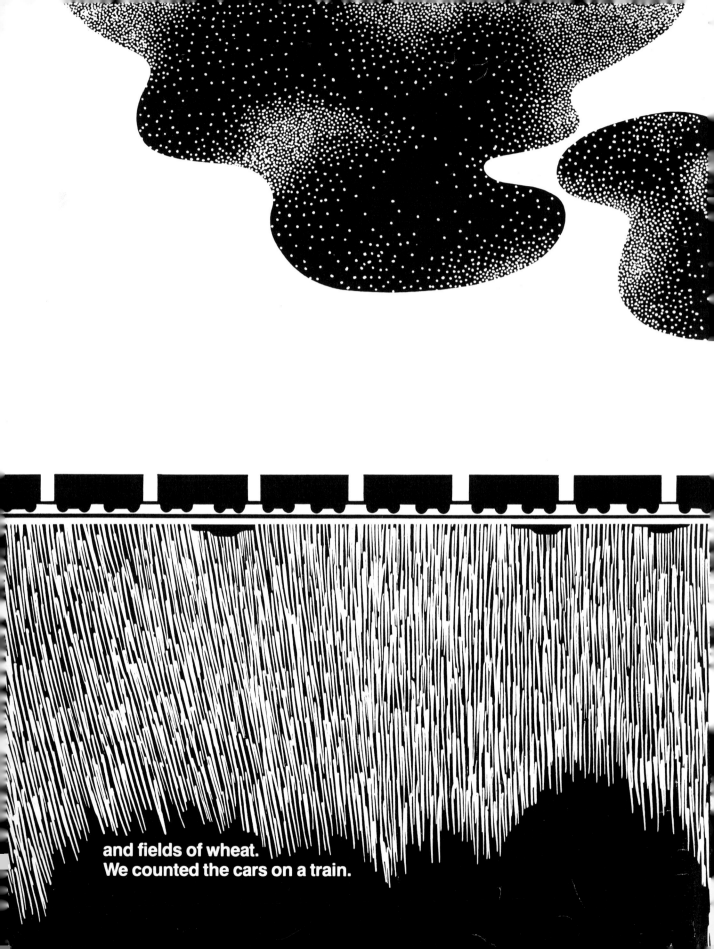

and fields of wheat.
We counted the cars on a train.

It rained hard
and puddles formed.

The road wound through the mountains.
Trails led into the woods.

Lightning flashed across the sky.

On the highway,
we headed for the coast.

We went under an expressway.

The water was rough, the waves high.

As the smoke from the fireworks drifted away
and the birds resettled in the trees, we drove on.

We followed the shore past marshy inlets and summer cottages.

We saw fireworks and stopped to watch.

Then we saw the city.

We looked back. Searchlights pierced the sky.

We crossed a bridge,

In the country, telephone poles lined the road.

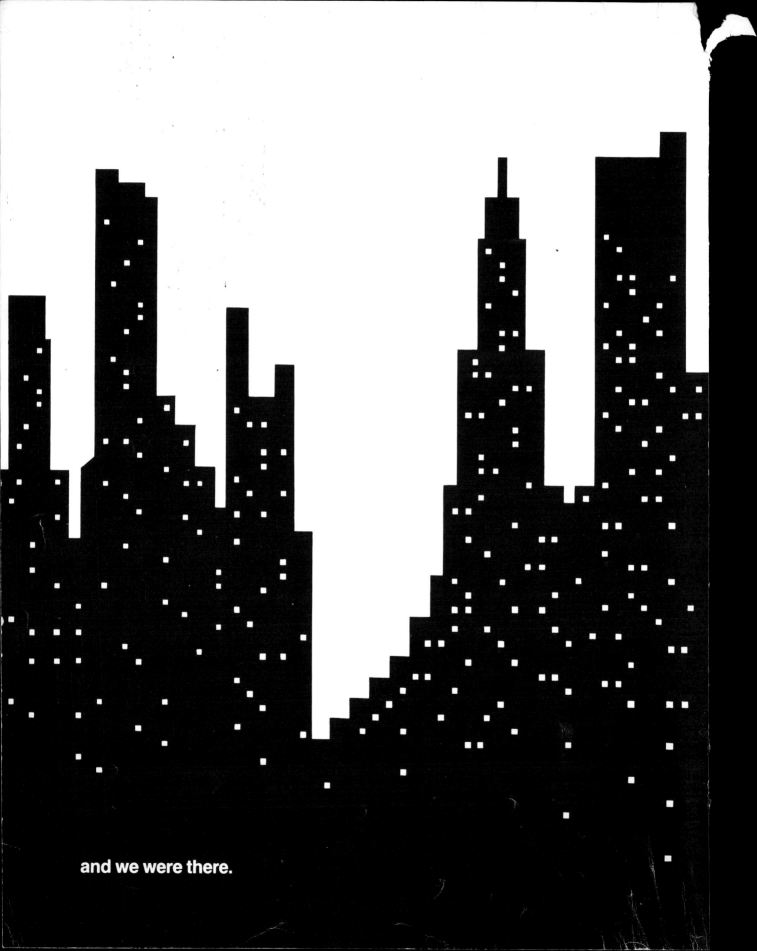

and we were there.

We left the shining, starlit city.

After parking the car, we rode the subway.

and picked up our car from the garage.

Then we went to a movie,

Then we had dinner in a restaurant,

and to the top of the tallest building.
We looked down.

Back on the street,
we looked up at where we had been.

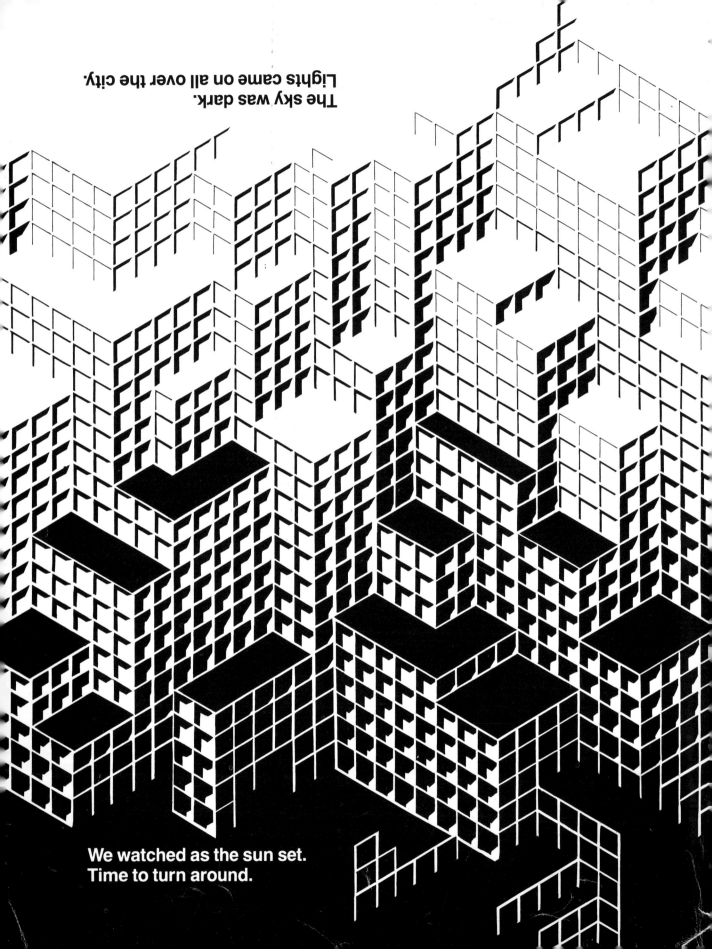

The sky was dark.
Lights came on all over the city.

We watched as the sun set.
Time to turn around.